JE

Gohmann, Johanna.

Spooky day at sea

1/21

-the-
PIRATE KIDS

A Spooky Day at Sea

BY Johanna Gohmann
ILLUSTRATED BY Jessika von Innerebner

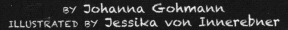

Calico Kid

An Imprint of Magic Wagon
abdopublishing.com

abdopublishing.com

Published by Magic Wagon, a division of ABDO, PO Box 398166, Minneapolis, Minnesota 55439. Copyright © 2018 by Abdo Consulting Group, Inc. International copyrights reserved in all countries. No part of this book may be reproduced in any form without written permission from the publisher. Calico Kid™ is a trademark and logo of Magic Wagon.

Printed in the United States of America, North Mankato, Minnesota.
092017
012018

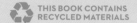

THIS BOOK CONTAINS
RECYCLED MATERIALS

Written by Johanna Gohmann
Illustrated by Jessika von Innerebner
Edited by Heidi M.D. Elston
Art Directed by Candice Keimig

Publisher's Cataloging-in-Publication Data

Names: Gohmann, Johanna, author. I von Innerebner, Jessika, illustrator.
Title: A spooky day at sea / by Johanna Gohmann; illustrated by Jessika von Innerebner.
Description: Minneapolis, Minnesota : Magic Wagon, 2018. I Series: The pirate kids
Summary: There's a storm at sea. Piper and Percy must stay below deck. The wind is blowing, and the thunder is loud. They decide to hide in a closet until the storm is over. But then Percy thinks he sees a pirate ghost in the closet with them! Piper and Percy are surprised when they realize the ghost is their father's pirate coat and hat hanging on a hook.
Identifiers: LCCN 2017946427 I ISBN 9781532130403 (lib.bdg.) I ISBN 9781532131004 (ebook) I ISBN 9781532131301 (Read-to-me ebook)
Subjects: LCSH: Pirates--Fiction--Juvenile fiction. I Brothers and sisters--Juvenile fiction. I Ghosts--Juvenile fiction. I Mistaken identity--Juvenile fiction.
Classification: DDC [E]--dc23
LC record available at https://lccn.loc.gov/2017946427

Table of Contents

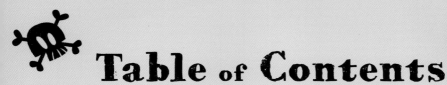

Chapter #1
A Very Bad Storm

Percy and Piper stand on the bow of the family pirate ship. They watch the gray, stormy water swirl below.

"It looks like the sky is moving even faster than we are!" Percy says. He points at the dark, puffy clouds racing overhead.

"I know! Mom said a really big storm is on the way," Piper says.

Just then, thunder rumbles in the distance.

"It feels kind of spooky," Percy whispers.

"Aye!" Piper agrees. "It reminds me of the Sea Spirit."

Percy looks at his sister with wide eyes. "What? I don't know that story."

"I can't tell you. You're too little," Piper says.

"I'm only one year younger than you!" Percy straightens his black eye patch and stands up tall. "Tell me! Please?"

"Well," Piper sighs. "Legend says when it storms at sea, it wakes up the Sea Spirit. He's a pirate ghost, and he likes to hide on pirate ships!"

"Oh please! That's just silly." Percy frowns. "That doesn't scare me. I'm not scared of anything!"

Just then, a big bolt of lightning streaks across the sky. Percy screams and wraps his arms around his sister.

"Yo ho ho!" Piper laughs.

"Argh, children!" their father calls to them. "Get below deck. The storm is picking up!"

Piper and Percy race to the ladder just as fat raindrops start to fall.

Chapter #2
Time to Hide

As the storm blows, Piper and Percy play their favorite board game, Capture the Booty. Their parents stay above deck steering the ship over the choppy water.

Percy is usually very good at Capture the Booty. But he is having a hard time paying attention.

BOOM! Goes the thunder. Percy jumps and accidentally knocks his game pieces off the board.

"Avast ye!" Piper says. "Stop being so lily-livered, brother. It's only a storm!"

Suddenly the ship tilts, and the rest of the game pieces roll across the floor. A porthole window blows open. Wind whooshes into the room.

"Argh!" Piper and Percy shout at the same time.

"Here, into the closet!" Piper says. She grabs a small lantern and pulls her brother inside. She closes the door behind them.

"This is a really bad storm! We'll hide out in here until it blows over," she says.

"Good idea," Percy says. He scoots closer to his sister. Outside, the wind continues to howl. "It sure is dark in here," he gulps.

"Here, let me see if I can turn up the lantern a bit," Piper says. She fidgets with the small lantern. The light gets a tiny bit brighter.

Percy looks around the closet. He can't believe his eyes. Standing in the back is a tall, dark figure in a long coat with a giant pirate hat.

"P-P-Piper?" Percy stammers.

"What is it now?" Piper asks.

"It's the Sea Spirit!"

Chapter #3
A Terrible Fright

Piper looks where Percy is pointing. She holds up the lantern to get a better look at the dark figure.

"Percy, don't be silly. That's only . . ." she starts to say. But much to her surprise, the figure moves one of its arms!

"Aaaaaaah!" Piper and Percy scream and accidentally blow out the lantern.

Suddenly, there is a rumble outside the closet. Then there's a loud bang against the closet door. Piper and Percy try to open the door, but it won't budge!

"Someone help us!" Percy yells.

The closet is very dark. Just then, Piper feels something lightly touch her shoulders. She lets out a loud yell.

"It's the ghost!" she shouts. "It's got me!"

The closet door suddenly bursts open. There stand Piper and Percy's mom and dad.

"What on earth is going on in here?" their mother asks.

"Argh!" their father says. "We hit rough seas. It looks like the piano rolled in front of the closet door. I'm so sorry you were trapped inside!"

Piper rushes out and throws her arms around her mother. "The ghost was trying to get me!" she says.

Chapter #4
The Secret of the Sea Spirit

"Ghost? What ghost?" Their mother looks confused. "Piper, my little lass, why are you wearing my winter scarf?"

Piper suddenly realizes she has her mother's scarf around her shoulders. It must have fallen off a hook in the closet!

Piper can't help but laugh. "Shiver me timbers! It was a scarf, not a ghost!"

"But we saw the Sea Spirit!" Percy insists.

Together, the family peers inside the closet. But all they see is a long winter coat and a pirate hat.

"It's just Dad's coat and hat, you squiffy," Piper says.

"Aye, Piper. No name-calling, please," their mother says.

"But I saw it move. I know I did." Percy walks into the closet. He pulls his dad's coat off the hook. Poppy the parrot is hiding inside!

Their father chuckles. "It looks like you two weren't the only ones afraid of the big storm!"

"Argh!" squawks Poppy. "Shiver me timbers!"

The whole family laughs. Percy is so relieved, he laughs loudest of all.

"Whew!" he says. "I was sure it was the Sea Spirit!"

"Sorry if I scared you with that story, brother," Piper says. "I got spooked as well!"

"That's okay," Percy says. "It was a creepy afternoon! But it was also kind of a fun adventure."

"That's enough spookiness for one day," their father says. "The storm has passed. Why don't you both head above deck now to play?"

31

"Great idea," Piper says. "You're it!"
She tags her brother and races away.

Percy scrambles up the ladder after
Piper. Outside, the sun is bright and
warm on his face. He's very glad the
storm is over!